grades preK-2

rea~~ding~~

My

n

Sound Box

by Jane Belk Moncure

illustrated by Linda Sommers

THE CHILD'S WORLD

ELGIN, ILLINOIS 60120

Distributed by Childrens Press, 1224 West Van Buren Street,
Chicago, Illinois 60607.

Library of Congress Cataloging in Publication Data

Moncure, Jane Belk.
  My n sound box.

  (Sound box books)
  SUMMARY: A little girl fills her sound box with many
words beginning with the letter "n".
  [1. Alphabet] I. Sommers, Linda. II. Title.
III. Series.
PZ7.M739Myn   [E]   78-22053
ISBN 0-89565-054-1

My ''n'' Sound Box

Little  had a box.

"I will find things that begin with my 'n' sound," she said.

"I will put them into my sound box."

Little ⬛ found a tree with nuts on it.

Little  climbed the tree. She picked nuts.

How many nuts?

8

Little n counted nine nuts.

She made the number 9.

Did she put the nine nuts and the number 9 into her box?

She did.

Next, Little  made nine groups of nuts.

How many nuts? Little  counted

ninety nuts. She made the number 90.

She put these nuts into her box with the other nuts. Now how many nuts did she have?

box

Little n counted ninety-nine nuts.

She made the number **99**.

Did she put the number 99 into her box?

She did.

Then Little 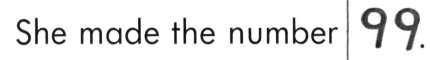 climbed the tree again.

Little  found nightingales,

nine nightingales
eating nuts!

When the nightingales saw

Little n, they flew into their nests.

Little n put the nightingales and their nests into her box, carefully . . .

because there were eggs in the nests.

Little n could not count how many.

Little  was sleepy.　So she took a nap.

The next day, Little  got out her piggy bank. She emptied out her nickels,

lots of nickels, 99 nickels!

21

Little  took her nickels to a store.

She bought a necklace for her mother

and a necktie for her father.

She also bought a nutcracker.

Little  n had 19 nickels left.

So she bought a nightgown for herself.

Little  carried all her new things home.
She put on her new nightgown.

Then she heard a noise. She looked into her
box and saw nineteen new nightingales.
They were crying for nuts!

"Don't cry," said Little  "I have enough nuts for all of you." She cracked some nuts.

nightingales

nests

nuts

Then, while the nightingales ate, she spread out her new things.

nightgown

necklace

nutcracker

necktie

Can you read these words with Little  ?

newspaper

nectarine

noodles

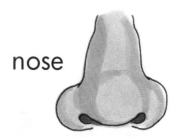

nose

notes

needle

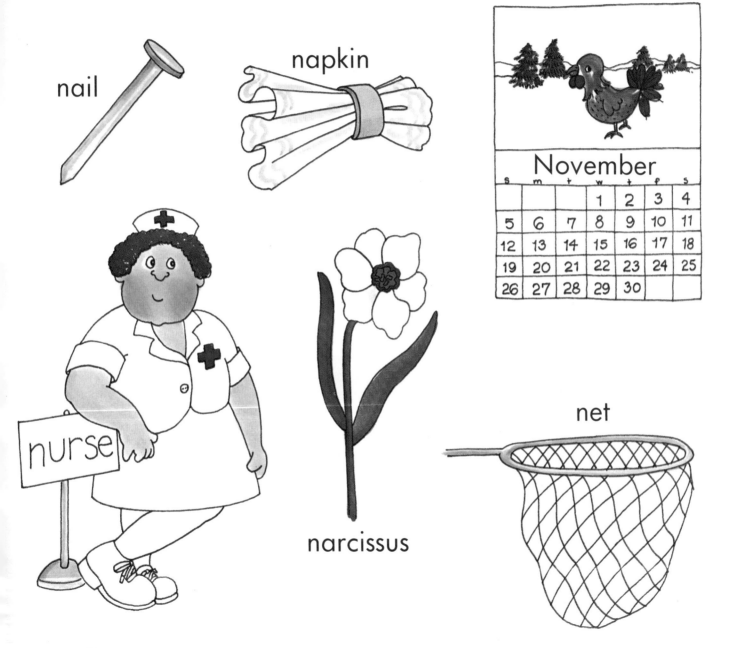

nail

napkin

November

s	m	t	w	t	f	s
				1	2	3	4
5	6	7	8	9	10	11
12	13	14	15	16	17	18
19	20	21	22	23	24	25
26	27	28	29	30		

nurse

narcissus

net

29

About the Author

Jane Belk Moncure, author of many books and stories for young children, is a graduate of Virginia Commonwealth University and Columbia University. She has taught nursery, kindergarten and primary children in Europe and America. Mrs. Moncure has taught early childhood education while serving on the faculties of Virginia Commonwealth University and the University of Richmond. She was the first president of the Virginia Association for Early Childhood Education and has been recognized widely for her services to young children. She is married to Dr. James A. Moncure, Vice President of Elon College, and currently teaches in Burlington, North Carolina.